Snow

written by Karen Hoenecke

KAEDEN BOOKS™

Table of Contents

Tree

pine tree

Snow is on the tree.

Car

Snow is actually clear. It looks white because of the way the sunlight reflects off of it.

Snow is on the car.

Fence

Snowflakes have six sides.

Snow is on the fence.

Sidewalk

Snow is on the **sidewalk.**

Patio

Snow is a form of precipitation. Othe forms of precipitati are rain, hail, and sleet.

Snow is on the **patio**.

Roof

Snow is on the roof.

Slide

Snow is on the slide.

Ground

Snow is on the ground.

Playhouse

Snow is on the playhouse.

Me

Snow is on me.

Everywhere

Snow is everywhere!

Glossary

patio – a paved or wood framed area next to a house that is used for dining and lounging

sidewalk – a hard walkway along the side of a road

snow – soft white bits of frozen water that fall from the sky in cold weather

Index